Moana
and the Sea

By Heather Knowles

Illustrated by Annette Marnat

Inspired by the film

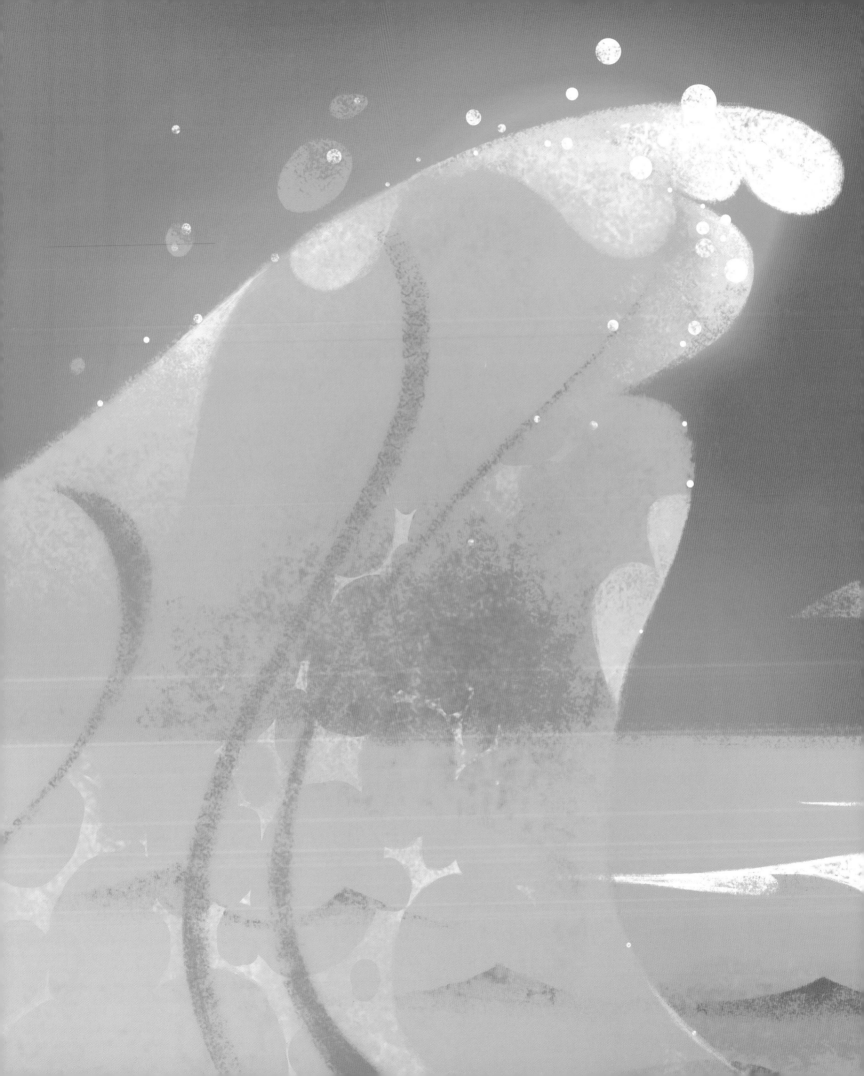

I am the **sea**, and I have known **Moana** since she was a little girl.

We spent our days together.
She played on the **sand** and
collected **shells** from my **shore**.

Moana was **fearless**, even then. She loved to **discover** and **explore** ..

... but her **heart** was always kind and full of **love**.

She **splashed** in my **waves.** We played together.

I felt her
curious spirit,

her sense of
adventure.

The years passed, and I watched

Moana grow.

I saw her take on
new challenges ...

... and make her village **proud.**

Every day, **Moana** learned.
She listened to her Gramma Tala.
She trusted her own **rhythm**.

Step by step,
she **climbed**
towards her **goals** ...

... and reached
wonderful heights.

One day, **Moana** decided to follow her **heart**.

She sailed out into the unknown. I felt her **determination**, her **courage**.

I saw her **try**.

I saw her struggle.

And when she failed,
I saw her cry.

But she never gave up.
She tried again.

She never forgot who she was.

She is special. She is brave.
She is my Moana.